This Notebook Belongs To :

From :

Made in the USA
Monee, IL
12 October 2021

79860130R00056